ANOTHER CHRISTMAS

SUSAN L. ROTH

MORROW JUNIOR BOOKS

NEW YORK

*The author would like to acknowledge
Lulu Delacre and El Museo del Barrio, New York.*

Mirador is a Spanish word for a lookout spot,
one with a wonderful view. In a Spanish-speaking land,
a hotel with a beautiful vista
might well be named Mirador.

The full-color artwork is a cut paper collage.
The text type is 15 point Chelmsford Medium.

Copyright © 1992 by Susan L. Roth

Printed in Hong Kong by South China Printing Company (1988) Ltd.

1   2   3   4   5   6   7   8   9   10

Library of Congress Cataloging-in-Publication Data
Roth, Susan L.
Another Christmas / Susan Roth.
p.   cm.
Summary: The year after Grandpa's death, Ben's family spends
Christmas in Puerto Rico, where Grandma makes sure the holiday still
has some familiar elements while being a little different.
ISBN 0-688-099942-4 (trade). — ISBN 0-688-09943-2 (library)
[1. Christmas—Fiction.   2. Puerto Rico—Fiction.
3. Grandmothers—Fiction.   4. Death—Fiction.]   I. Title.
PZ7.R737An   1992
[E]—dc20   91-33148   CIP   AC

For Ben, this is Christmas: the whole family together in the still, icy cold; skating, sledding, snowmen—the hills white as far as you can see; chopping down the Christmas tree—Ben and Grandpa always do that together; and Grandma baking, baking. Ben cuts out the gingerbread men. When they're done, the cookies wait in a row for chilly hands. Spicy cider is in the air and there's singing in the kitchen.

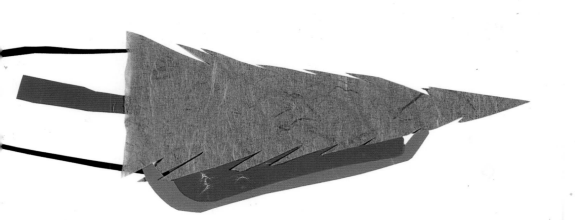

But last spring, Grandpa died. Now the hills are white again, only how can Christmas come if Grandpa isn't here?

"Maybe we could try to make this a different sort of Christmas," Mama says quietly.

"How about a hot Christmas instead of a cold one?" says Dad. "Let's go to Puerto Rico."

"There's no snow in Puerto Rico," Grandma says. "That's no Christmas."

"But we've never been anywhere for Christmas except home," says Dad.

And Mama adds, "We all need to get far away."

"What about chopping down the tree?" asks Ben. "What about cold nights with Grandma's quilts wrapped around us? What about snow?"

"If Dad and Mama think we should get away, then maybe we should," says Grandma. "We'll still be together no matter where we are."

No more talking—and they pack up their summer things.

The snow blows sideways on the little windows and the plane shivers as it climbs to blue skies. Soon enough a turquoise sea stretches to meet them. There it is, Puerto Rico. No snow.

"Here we are," says Dad. "A pink and yellow village, a bright turquoise beach, a little family inn."

And Mama says, "Imagine, it was snowing when we left. Feel how hot it is here. Let's go change and look for shells on the beach."

"You go find shells," Grandma says. "Take a swim. But Ben and I, we'll walk through the little pink and yellow village after we put on our summer clothes." Grandma holds Ben's hand and Ben holds hers.

They wander into the village. Mary, Joseph, and the Baby Jesus sit as big as real people in front of a little pink church.

"Ben, remember where Christmas started?" says Grandma. "Bethlehem. No snow."

"No snow, like here," says Ben. "But Grandma, see that hill? It looks like snow."

"Looks like snow, Ben, but I think it's flowers. Tiny white ones."

"I still wish it were snow."

"Me, too, Ben, but I have a snowy Christmas secret."

"What?" says Ben.

"I'm not telling," says Grandma. Her eyes crinkle at the sides. "Not telling yet."

They stop in front of a dusty yellow store full of carved wooden figures. An old man sits inside, painting a tiny rooster red.

"Look at the Three Kings," Ben says softly. "They're sitting on horses instead of camels. Look at that Baby Jesus." Baby Jesus is wooden and stiff, with arms stretched straight out. "Look at that man putting a rooster into the manger."

"Special in Puerto Rico, special for Christmas," the old man says.

"For Christmas." Grandma's eyes look shiny. "Let's take them all. It's Christmas here, too." She holds Ben's hand a little tighter.

"Feliz Navidad," says the old man. "That means Merry Christmas."

"Merry Christmas," they say in soft voices. *"Feliz Navidad."*

Ben holds the red rooster by its foot—it's still wet—and they stop in front of a little pink store. Wild dancing music spills out onto the sidewalk.

"What about some Christmas music?" says Grandma.

"Is *this* Christmas music?" asks Ben.

"I don't know what this is," says Grandma. "But let's buy a Puerto Rican Christmas tape."

"Why?" Ben asks. "We can't play it."

"Don't be so sure," says Grandma.

"Why?" says Ben.

"You'll see." Grandma's eyes crinkle again. "You'll see."

At the corner, Christmas trees are for sale, pine trees, just like home.

"What do you think?" says Grandma.

"Pretty tiny," says Ben.

"They don't grow here; it's too hot," says Grandma. "Maybe they were shipped from home."

"We could have had our own tree from the woods in back of your house. I could have chopped it down, even without Grandpa helping."

"This is our tree now," says Grandma.

They go back to the turquoise beach, to the little hotel.

Grandma opens the door to her room. "Here's my secret," she says.

"It's cold!" says Ben. "It's freezing cold in here."

"Just like home," says Grandma. "I turned up the air conditioning as far as it would go."

Ben laughs.

"Close those pink curtains, hide that turquoise beach for a while," says Grandma. She stands the tree in the yellow wastebasket. She sets it on top of the little pink table.

"Here's some more of my secret," says Grandma. She opens her suitcase and takes out a red box. "You need this because it's so cold."

Ben puts on the green woolly sweater and smiles into the mirror.

"Thank you, Grandma. I like your secret!"

"Just part of my secret," says Grandma. "Now listen." She takes out a little tape recorder, pushes a button, and the room is full of Christmas carols.

"Look," Grandma says. She pulls out candy canes, tinsel garlands, shiny balls, all red and green.

"You brought our Christmas with us, Grandma." Ben's eyes crinkle like hers.

Now Grandma takes out a box stuffed with puffs of tissue paper. "Careful," she whispers.

Ben drops tissue papers on the floor one at a time. In the middle is a Christmas angel, Grandpa's angel, the one from every other Christmas since Grandpa was a boy. Grandpa always held Ben up so he could put it on the very top of the tree.

Ben hugs the angel and starts to cry. Grandma puts her arms all around him.

"You'll still put the angel on the very top. We're lucky.
I thought you'd have to put it on the top of a palm tree!"
    Ben and Grandma twist the tinsel garlands around the
tree. They hook on every candy cane and hang up every
shining ball. Ben puts the Christmas angel on the very top,
and the tree leans over a little, but it's still beautiful.

Grandma pulls out one more box, full of gingerbread men.

"That's all my secret, Ben," says Grandma.

Ben bites off a head. "Very good secret," he says.

Ben and Grandma arrange the Nativity scene with the red rooster standing near Baby Jesus. The Three Kings are on horses, Puerto Rican–style, but they're still the same kings— Caspar, Melchior, and Balthazar.

Grandma plays the Puerto Rican Christmas tape.

"This sounds like the dancing music we heard on the street," says Ben.

"No silent night tonight in Puerto Rico," says Grandma. *"Feliz Navidad, Ben."*

"How can *Feliz Navidad* just mean Merry Christmas if the music is this jumpy?" asks Ben.

"It's still Merry Christmas," says Grandma, "only a little different from the Christmas we know."

"A little different," says Ben. His feet are moving.

"A little different," says Grandma. She takes his hands.

There's a knock at the door. It's Mama and Dad.
"What's all this?" Mama smiles.
"Grandma brought Christmas in her suitcase!" says Ben.
"But she didn't bring this music! I can hardly keep my feet still." Dad is smiling, too.

And two thousand miles from the snowy white hills, at the turquoise beach baking in the sun, Ben and Grandma, Mama and Dad, all start to celebrate another Christmas.